Young Heroes

THE KIDNAPPING

Ann Harth

Dion Hamill

RISING STARS

First published in the UK by
Rising Stars UK Ltd.
7 Hatchers Mews, Bermondsey Street, London SE1 3GS
www.risingstars-uk.com

This edition published 2011

Text © UC Publishing Pty Ltd.
www.ucpublishing.com

First published 2006 by Insight Publications Pty Ltd.
ABN 57 005 102 983,
89 Wellington Street,
St Kilda, Victoria 3182
Australia

Development: UC Publishing Pty Ltd
Cover design: UC Publishing/Design Ed
Written by: Ann Harth
Illustrations: Dion Hamill
Text design and typesetting: Design Ed/Clive Sutherland
Editorial consultancy: Dee Reid

British Library Cataloguing in Publication Data.
A CIP record for this book is available from the British Library.

ISBN: 978-1-84680-807-4

Printed by Craft Print International Ltd., Singapore

Contents

Chapter 1
David's in trouble

Jemma's little boat rocked and wobbled as the speedboat sped past. Water splashed over the edge and covered her feet. The motor stopped.

'Oh no,' she said. 'Not again!' She pulled the rope on the motor. Nothing happened.

The boy in the speedboat waved. His name was David Holland. David's father was the richest man in town.

Jemma watched David Holland speed towards a big fishing trawler. When he got there, he slowed down.

Jemma saw two men on the trawler's deck.
They were waving and yelling.

'Their motor must have stopped too,'
Jemma thought. 'David will try to help them.'

She watched David tie up his speedboat next to the trawler and climb up a rope ladder.

The men pulled David onto the deck.

Jemma turned back to her motor. She got out a screwdriver from her tool bag. She turned one of the screws. Then she pulled the rope as hard as she could. This time the motor started. She wanted to get to shore before it stopped again. It was a long way to paddle. She looked back at the trawler one more time.

Wait! What was happening? The men were holding David's arms. It looked as if David was trying to pull away. The dog barked in the speedboat below.

'Help! Let me go!' cried David.

David Holland was in trouble.

Jemma turned her boat around. She went round the back of the trawler. The men wouldn't see her there. Jemma stopped her motor when she was near the trawler.

Her boat floated quietly. Jemma saw a fishing net hanging over the side. She took out a paddle and rowed over to the net. Then she tied her boat to the net. She heard voices.

'Make it tight, Bart,' a man said.

Then Jemma heard David's voice. 'Stop! You're hurting me.'

Jemma held her breath. What was happening? She listened.

'I'm surprised your father lets you go out alone, David,' the man said. 'Someone could kidnap you. I bet Daddy would pay a lot of money to get you back.'

'Ow!' David said.

The man spoke again. 'Not too tight, Bart. We don't want to hurt him unless we have to.'

Jemma's boat bumped into the trawler. David's dog heard the noise. It gave a bark.

Chapter 2
Stump floats away

'Shut that dog up!' said one of the men to David.

'Shhh. Quiet, Stump!' David called.

Stump barked louder. He jumped into the air and landed with a thud on the bottom of the speedboat.

'Hey Rodney, maybe the little dog wants to go for a swim,' Bart said.

'No!' David yelled.

Bart climbed down the ladder. He had a large knife. When Bart reached the speedboat, Stump growled. Then he jumped up and caught Bart's trousers in his teeth.

'Hey! Get off!' Bart yelled. He shook his leg and Stump fell back into the boat. Bart cut the rope between the boats and pushed the speedboat away with his foot.

Stump grew quiet and sat down as the speedboat drifted towards the bow of the trawler.

'You can't just let him go. He'll die!' Jemma heard David yell.

'Come on. We've got work to do,' said Bart. 'Tie the kid up and throw away his keys. We don't want him getting any bright ideas.'

Jemma heard footsteps, a splash, then more footsteps.

Then Jemma saw David's speedboat floating by. Stump was sitting at the front. She hoped he wouldn't bark at her or they would both be in trouble.

Jemma listened hard. She couldn't hear the men. They must have gone into the cabin.

Good. Maybe she could rescue Stump.

The speedboat came closer. Jemma reached her hand towards it, but it was too far away. She picked up her paddle and tried again.

Stump stood up.

'It's OK, Stump,' Jemma said softly. 'Be very quiet so I can help you.' She touched the edge of the speedboat with the paddle and pulled it towards her.

Stump barked. Jemma froze.

Chapter 3
Saving Stump

How could Jemma keep Stump quiet? Even if she rescued David, they couldn't escape in the speedboat. The keys were gone. Jemma had to get Stump into her boat.

Stump barked again. Jemma thought the men would hear Stumnp. She looked up at the trawler. No one was there.

Jemma turned back to Stump. Then she saw something at the bottom of her boat. It was her lunch! She hoped Stump liked peanut butter. Jemma quickly picked up a sandwich and broke off a bit. She pulled the speedboat closer and held out her sandwich.

Stump sniffed at it and wagged his tail.

'Come on, boy. Jump in,' she said softly.

Stump moved closer.

'Come on,' Jemma said again.

Stump jumped into Jemma's boat.

'Good boy,' Jemma said. She patted his head and gave him the sandwich.

Jemma tied the speedboat to the trawler. Stump sat quietly and ate the rest of Jemma's lunch.

'Now we have to save David,' Jemma said. Stump wagged his tail.

How could Jemma get onto the deck? She looked at the fishing net hanging over the side of the trawler. She moved closer and pulled on it. It seemed strong.

'You wait here, Stump,' Jemma whispered. 'I'll be back.' She tied her tool belt around her waist and climbed up the net.

Chapter 4
A plan

Jemma pulled herself onto the deck and hid behind a pile of boxes. She looked around. The men were inside the cabin. David was tied up. Jemma could see an open trap door. She could also see a ladder. The engine must be down there.

Jemma had an idea. 'Hey,' she whispered.

David looked up.

'Act as if you can't hear me,' Jemma whispered again. She looked at the men in the cabin. 'They can see you.'

She crept towards David, staying behind the boxes. She got as close as she could.

'Can you hear me?' she whispered. 'Blink if you can.'

David blinked.

'I'm going to cut you free,' Jemma whispered.

David blinked. The men were still in the cabin. One was talking on the phone. He sounded angry.

Jemma took a deep breath. She took her knife from her tool belt and crawled across the floor. She reached up to cut David's ropes. His wrists were bleeding.

'Don't move yet. Wait until I tell you,' she whispered.

David wiggled his fingers. He kept his hands behind him.

Jemma looked towards the trap door. It seemed far away. She couldn't see the men in the cabin, but David could.

'When you're sure they're not looking, tap your foot,' Jemma whispered.

Jemma waited. She squeezed the knife in her hand and felt sweat drip down her face.

David's foot moved.

Tap, tap, tap.

Jemma didn't wait. She was too afraid to look towards the cabin. She slid across the deck on her stomach. She reached the trap door and climbed down the ladder.

It was very dark in the engine room. Then her eyes got used to the dark. She found the fuel tank. A hose ran from the tank to the engine. Jemma cut it.

'That'll stop you,' she said.

THAT'LL STOP YOU.

Chapter 5
Escape

Jemma climbed up the ladder and looked out. David watched her.

'Ready?' she whispered.

'Ready,' David whispered back. Jemma climbed onto the deck as David jumped up. They raced forward. David was ahead.

'Hey!' Bart and Rodney ran from the cabin.

David climbed over the rail and dropped into the boat. Jemma was right behind him. She threw her leg over the edge and grabbed the net. She started to climb down.

'Ow!' Jemma felt a sharp pain. Bart had a handful of her hair. She was caught.

Bart's hand grabbed her arm. Then he let go of her hair. Jemma opened her mouth. She bit Bart's hand as hard as she could. Bart yelled and let go of Jemma's arm. She dropped into the boat.

Jemma cut the rope that tied her boat to the trawler.

'Push us away!' she yelled. David grabbed a paddle and pushed against the side of the trawler.

Jemma looked up as she pulled the rope on her motor. Bart was climbing down the net. He had almost reached the bottom.

Jemma's motor didn't start.

'Don't do this to me now!' Jemma yelled. She thumped the motor with her fist and pulled one more time. It started. They moved away from the trawler.

Chapter 6
Almost safe

Jemma's eyes opened wide as she heard the trawler's engine starting.

'I thought you fixed the engine so it wouldn't work,' David said.

'I cut the fuel line,' Jemma said. 'It will still work until the fuel in the line is used up.'

'How long will that be?' David said.

'I don't know,' Jemma said.

She steered them away from the trawler. They were moving, but not very fast. The trawler turned towards them. It came closer and closer without slowing down.

'They're going to run over us!' David yelled. 'We have to jump.' He grabbed Stump's collar.

Jemma raised her hand. 'Wait,' she said. 'Listen.'

The trawler's engine sounded different. It was slowing down.

Jemma smiled as she saw the two men waving their fists at them from the deck.

'It worked!' David shouted. 'We're safe!'

Stump barked and put his paws on David's lap.

Jemma turned her boat towards shore.

Fat drops of rain splashed into the ocean. The water was rough. Jemma looked into the sky. It was dark.

'We need to get to shore before this storm hits,' David said.

'Don't worry,' said Jemma. 'We can make it.'